Little Christmases

— short stories for the holidays —

by L. Phillips Carlson

Little Christmases, short stories for the holidays
by L. Phillips Carlson

Copyright © 2014 by L. Phillips Carlson

First print edition

Published by:
Snowsnake Press
PO Box 51732
Albuquerque NM 87181

Available on Kindle and other devices

Cover photo, "Santa Snow Globe" by Lee Jordan on Flickr
http://fotopedia.com/items/flickr-318007886
(adapted with attribution-share alike license
http://creativecommons.org/licenses/by-sa/2.0/)

Cover design, interior design, interior illustrations and text by
L. Phillips Carlson

Little Christmases and *Where is Christmas?* are works of fiction and
come from the imagination of the author. Any resemblance to
actual events or persons living or deceased is purely
coincidental. *A Kind Word in a Strange Land* and *Christmas Timber*
are fictionalized memoirs from the author's life. Characters'
names and some details have been changed.

A version of the first story originally appeared as *Little
Christmases Along the Way* in Christian Single, Dec. 1997.

Acknowledgements

I've got the greatest critique buddies in the world! Thank you to authors Kathlena L. Contreras (K. Lynn Bay) and Lara LaVonne Jordan for your critical eye and good advice. Thank you, also, to Lori Johnson and Wendy Bickel, wonderful writers who are good friends and offer all kinds of support.

And a huge thank you to my family, especially my husband. I didn't use your real names so no one needs to know about the whole tree thing—unless they read the last story in here. So, you're safe for now—shhh!

Table of Contents

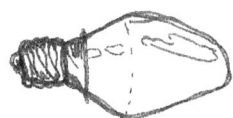

Little Christmases

Cook dinner? Forget it. I ordered pizza.

All day long I'd struggled with last-minute Christmas errands and in the process wrapped myself into a very bad mood. I'd languished in long lines at the post office, burdened with armloads of packages. I'd pushed my way through the too-crowded mall, vainly searching for the right brands, colors, and styles. Everything appeared so fake, from gaudy window displays of toothy elves to tarnished garlands of red and green. My Christmas spirit died bit by bit as choruses of "Bah, humbug!" seemed to come from every corner.

The pizza came. As I stuffed a cold, soggy piece in my mouth, I glanced at my Christmas tree. I'd bought it only two days ago, but the branches were already beginning to droop.

That figures.

Suddenly something wiggled deep in the branches. *What now?* I wondered. Who knew what might have crawled into it at the tree lot?

Peering closer, I saw a tiny figure opening and closing its wings like a butterfly. I rubbed my eyes and tried to focus more clearly. It looked like a very small angel, dressed in gleaming white, with soft, feathery wings. She performed a quick pirouette and sat down on a nearby satin ball ornament. Her sweet face glowed in the light of a blinking bulb.

Then she looked right at me.

"You're missing them," she said.

"Huh?" I felt my mouth fall open.

"I said, you're missing them."

I shook my head. "Missing what?"

"All the little Christmases," she said, fluffing her wings. "You had two today."

I frowned. "I don't understand."

"They're the nice little things that happen to you every day," the angel said, adjusting her halo. "Little Christmases."

"Nothing nice happened to me today," I said, a bit too crossly.

The angel stopped preening and put on a serene smile. "Oh, you're quite wrong. What about the girl behind you in line at the post office who lent you her pen?"

I had forgotten about that.

The angel pursed her lips. "The pen's still in your handbag. You forgot to give it back."

Oops.

"Then there was the guy at the mall—the one with the ponytail and the earring? He held the door open for you."

That I remembered. "Yeah, and then he muttered

something under his breath."

The angel tilted her head slightly. "He said, 'God bless you.'"

Uh, oh!

Had I been in such a foul mood that I missed these simple courtesies, these small acts of kindness? Hadn't I been taught to treat others like I wanted to be treated?

I suddenly recalled snarling at a clerk when she didn't answer quickly enough. I had to look away from the angel.

"That's OK," she said, as if reading my thoughts. "You did a little Christmas yourself."

"I did?"

"Sure. You told the pizza boy to keep the change."

"Big deal," I answered. "It was $9.95 total, with tip."

"Yes, but you gave him a twenty by mistake."

That's why his eyes got so big! I remembered the kid—tall, gawky, bad complexion. And torn jeans, not the stylish kind.

I thought for a moment. Any kid working around Christmastime probably needed the money a lot more than I did.

"You need to be more observant," the angel said quietly. She stood up and smoothed out her small dress. "Christmas is more than ripping open presents. You should have a hundred little Christmases before you get to that point, both ones you give and ones you receive."

I shrugged. "There's only a couple days left before

December 25."

"They're there. You just have to look for them." The angel leapt to another branch and balanced herself on top of a candy cane. She gave me a knowing smile. Then, with a swift flick of her wings, she quickly disappeared into the thick midsection of the tree.

A strange peace filled me. Maybe I would be able to enjoy this Christmas, after all. The harried world seemed far away as I thought about the real meaning behind the holiday, about being kind to each other, and about little Christmases.

I looked at my tree again. It didn't look so droopy, after all.

A Kind Word in a Strange Land

Christmas 1979 was a very lonely time for me. My husband's company relocated us from sunny New Mexico to the wilds of Washington D.C. for a one-year stint of technical advising, and I didn't know a soul. I finally made some friends, but it wasn't easy in a big, impersonal suburb.

But, almost from the start, our next-door neighbors made us feel comfortable. Like a spare mom and pop, an elderly Jewish couple named Sam and Charlotte took a liking to us and offered their help.

"Watch out for the silverfish," Charlotte warned, referring to the pesky damp-climate insects on my ceiling. "Have management spray before there are too many."

Commiseration is a wonderful thing in a strange land.

With my husband's work being so hectic, we tried to get away as often as possible and take weekend trips around that historical area. Sam would dutifully pick up the mail and newspaper for us—it was never a problem. Both he and Charlotte would be quick to suggest dry cleaners or other necessary stores or services. Since they'd lived in the area for years, it was quite helpful.

Thanksgiving rolled around, and I decided to try making a complete turkey dinner. We'd been married about six years, but I'd relied on going home to Mom and Dad's for most of those. Charlotte introduced me to a turkey rack, a special cooking device that forms a 'V' to hold a large bird. "Cook it upside down for the first hour," she instructed, "then the breast meat never gets too dry." Her method worked perfectly! I still cook turkeys this way.

Christmas came swiftly afterwards, as it always does. There was no going home that year, so a tree seemed in order. I located a nearby Christmas tree farm and set out to find the perfect tree. All they had were prickly Scotch pines, and small ones at that. I sawed one down best I could, threw it in my pickup truck, and later dragged it up three flights of steps. The tree, at four and one-half feet, looked miserably short. I grabbed a large packing box and covered it with a white sheet, then set the hapless tree on top of it. Our sparse decorations hung only in the front, but Charlotte declared it "Bee-yoo-tiful!" as only an East Coast accent can say it. She told me she particularly liked it because they never had a tree, since they celebrated Hanukkah instead.

And when Hanukkah began, Charlotte had us over for potato pancakes and to have a look at her special menorah. We shared laughter and memories as well. She produced pictures of a handsome Sam in his WWII uniform, and one of her with youthful good looks. They still had the glow of those earlier smiles.

After we moved back home to New Mexico, I sent her Christmas cards with yearly updates and a "Happy Hanukkah" scrawled on the bottom. She'd send me a Hanukkah card with a wobbly "Merry Christmas."

Then, sadly, one year Charlotte wrote that Sam had died. She soon moved to California to be near her daughter. After a few years, my cards eventually came back stamped with "Addressee Unknown," and I lost contact. Most likely, Charlotte, who was elderly when I met her, had passed on.

Sam and Charlotte were sweet and accepting. We shared our traditions easily, none of us feeling like we needed to abandon our own ways. We simply felt the joy of each other, as friends do.

So, Sam and Charlotte, wherever the universe has taken you, Happy Hanukkah *and* Merry Christmas. I miss you.

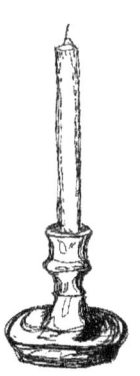

Christmas Timber

Finding a Christmas tree is supposed to be fun. Visions of old holiday cards come to mind, the ones illustrating happy people and a huge tree carried in a horse-drawn sleigh. Or those cards with a golden glow that show homemade cranberry and popcorn strings and glittery ornaments that go on the tree almost by themselves, all while the family sips punch and sings carols in four-part harmony.

And then, there's reality.

We quit cutting our own in the National Forest after the one time we got lost and hauled the tree for hours until we found the road again. So we resorted to finding trees in city lots. But, invariably, one of the kids wouldn't like the tree that the rest of us liked. Daughter Michelle had such a fit about one we chose a few years ago that she actually bought her own two-foot tree. Now she just buys her own mini-tree as a matter of rebellious tradition.

So it seemed heaven-sent when we actually found a tree the whole family liked. It was one of the first we saw as we entered the lot, but all four of us — my husband Dean, teenagers Michelle and Richard, and me — instinctively drew to it.

"It's a noble fir, 'bout ten or eleven foot," the parka-wearing attendant said. "Sixty-five dollars."

It sounded like a bargain since last year we paid almost a hundred. Tall trees don't come cheap. And noble firs smell so good.

Sold!

Michelle, even though she said she liked the big tree, purchased her own two-footer. Tradition is hard to break, after all.

We paid for the big tree and a wiry guy began to pull it out of the ground. I gasped when I noticed the trunk. It must have been at least eight inches across. Hadn't we made this mistake before?

My husband and the man lugged the tree to the Camry and tied it down on the roof. The branches draped over the windows and doors, making it hard to get in. But we managed; and along with Michelle's mini-tree, off we went.

Yes, in Christmases past, we had mistakenly purchased trees that were too big. It wasn't completely our fault. We had an empty dining room with a tall ceiling that, once we cleared out the accumulated junk, made a perfect place for a Christmas room. A big tree filled the space and made it look fabulous. It only made sense to think big.

One year we brought a heavy piñon home. Inside the house, its massive branches relaxed so much that we couldn't get it out the door after Christmas. We had to cut it apart right there in the carpeted dining room and then it took forever to vacuum out the needles and sawdust. Another year, we got a pretty "farm tree," a Scotch pine with a fat trunk that didn't fit our regular stand. I ended up frantically searching half-a-dozen stores before finding a stand that said it was especially made for big trees. It had worked fine, and I even knew where it was, should we need it now.

We headed home with our prize, driving at a speed of 15 miles per hour on a major thoroughfare and annoying other drivers. My goodness! Couldn't they see THE TREE? We certainly could, out any of the windows of the Camry. Each turn we took, the tree rolled slightly in the opposite direction. Fortunately, the rights and lefts more or less equaled each other as we wound up the hills to our house.

It took three of us — Dean, Richard and me — to lift the tree off the car and carry it to the garage, where, after much ceremonial measuring and head-scratching, a cut was made. Then we three again tried to carry it through the front door, held open by Michelle.

"You're stepping on the tree! I can hear it ripping!" Dean grunted.

I set my end down rather abruptly. The boys then decided they could carry it without me. "Fine," I said through gritted teeth. I didn't feel well anyway, having fought a nasty bronchitis for a couple of weeks.

While they messed with the tree, I got the "big"

stand ready. A heavy-duty affair, it consisted of a steel chain, four sinewy cables, a large pan and unclear directions. The boys righted the tree while I crawled underneath to fasten it together.

The tree's lushness made seeing difficult. Needles poked my arms and sap dripped on my sweater. I had to lie in a very awkward, stomach-down position as I reached and pulled and tightened everything.

I emerged from under the tree and judged its straightness. Dean, left holding the tree, looked like he was ready to die of boredom. "A little to the left," I said. "Nope, too far; now toward the living room; hold it!" and then dove under the tree again to make the final adjustments. Finally, it was anchored.

It was then we noticed a serious flaw: our perfect tree had not been trimmed properly while it'd been growing. The branches on one side were longer than the other, giving it a pregnant appearance. And just like its human counterpart, its balance was thrown off.

"This isn't working!" I said. At this point, I wished we'd gotten some scrawny native pine.

"Let me try," Richard said, always eager to solve such problems. "Where are the spare pieces of wood?"

Some small pieces of wood were packed with our regular-size tree stand. The old stand's screws often dug into the bark of soft trees, so the wood pieces helped to spread the stress. Richard found the chips and began to insert them under the trunk.

"Whoa, wait a minute!" I said. "We're not going to have this thing sitting on an unstable pile of woodchips."

"Well," Dean said, "it was a real pain to cut it the first time and haul it in here. How about we just use a couple of pieces?"

I sighed. "OK, but let me finish tightening everything." After tugging at the unyielding cables and tearing a fingernail, I again crawled out from underneath. "Let go," I ordered, "but get ready to catch."

The big tree lurched slightly and paused. I held my breath.

It stood.

"Yea!" Dean said brightly. "Let's get the decorations!"

"Let's wait and see if it's still standing tomorrow," I said, frowning.

The tree stood naked for several tomorrows as we busied ourselves with end-of-the-semester activities. I eventually put on the lights, the tree threatening to move at each touch.

In spite of its good looks, I just didn't trust this tree. I walked over and closed my thumb and forefinger around the tip of a needled branch. A slight tug produced an impressive sway, the tree righting itself after a couple of back and forth motions. Not good.

"We're not putting any breakable ornaments on the tree this year," I said, not sure anyone was listening.

After a couple more days of hanging an ornament

here, another ornament there, we decided enough was enough. We hadn't used more than half of what we normally put on, but it was getting close to Christmas and we needed to finish. And yes, we hung a few fragile ones since it just isn't Christmas without them.

My bronchitis got worse instead of better, even with antibiotics. A few nights before Christmas I dosed myself on both flu and cough medicine, hoping against hope to get a little sleep. It wasn't smart, but it worked. I was really zonked.

The kids took advantage of the holiday and stayed up late that night, playing computer games. Like most parents of teenagers, we said goodnight and let them exhaust themselves.

I drifted off into a medicated sleep. I'd been out for a couple of hours when I thought I heard something stirring in the room.

"Mom! Dad!" It was Michelle's voice. "The tree fell down!"

We roused ourselves—me, drunk on medicine and Dean, heavy with sleep—and made our way downstairs in our pajamas. Nightmare visions flashed through my head: a broken window, gouged drywall, or curtain rods ripped off the wall. What horrible things awaited?

We ran into the dining room. Yup, there was the huge tree, lying on its side. By some stroke of luck, though, it fell in the only place where it did no harm: diagonally across the room toward the kitchen. The top of the tree lay less than a couple of inches from the wall.

"Man, I didn't hear anything," I said.

"We heard the ornaments as it fell," Michelle said, standing near the kitchen door. "There was a thump and then a kind of tinkling sound."

We stood there, stupidly starting at the sideways tree.

"I unplugged the lights," Richard said, pointing to the wall outlet. "I thought it'd be safer."

Good, good. I looked at Dean. He didn't seem any more alert than I was.

"Um, Mom?" Michelle asked. "Shouldn't we get towels or something?"

It was only then I noticed the soaked rug. Of course, the extra-capacity stand had spilled on my recently-cleaned carpet. "Oh, yeah. Towels," I muttered. I really didn't want to deal with this right now.

Michelle and I mopped up as we discussed what to do. It didn't make sense to set it back up, since it took us more than an hour to do it last time and it'd probably just fall down again. Michelle put a fresh towel near the stand. It was then that I noticed a bend in the steel legs.

Perfect for large trees, the package had read. So much for truth in advertising. "The stand's broken." I said.

Dean shook his head. "Well, we can't set it up then. Let's go back to bed."

I nodded. "It's not going anywhere. And whatever ornaments are broken, it's too late now to do anything about it."

Morning came and I found Michelle removing the last of the ornaments." "Thank you, honey," I said, "I really appreciate all the work you did."

"Oh, it wasn't so bad," she said. "The tree threw most of them off." By some miracle, none of the ornaments broke and none of the light strings tore.

We still didn't have any new ideas of what to do. It was too close to Christmas to get a new tree that looked decent, and besides, we'd have wasted the $65.

"We could set it outside for the birds, and just not have a tree," I suggested.

No one liked that.

"We could put Michelle's mini-tree in here," Dean said, provoking giggles as we pictured our many presents beneath a two-foot tree in the otherwise empty room.

I shook my head. "We could just leave it sideways." But even for our family, that was a little too weird.

Dean poked through the midsection of the tree. "I know! Let's use the old stand."

"The trunk has to be smaller than a 6-inch diameter to fit," I said. I knew these things.

He jabbed a little deeper in the branches. "The tree is really full all over. We could just cut a couple feet off the bottom, up to where the trunk is about that size. It'd still be a nice tree, just shorter."

It seemed like the only thing to do.

It still wasn't easy. We sawed off several bottom branches, the sawdust again disappearing into the carpet. Then we measured carefully and made another couple of cuts, removing a veritable log from the bottom of the tree. Again, the pregnant profile made it impossible to figure a flat cut, but we wedged a firm scrap under the trunk and another block of wood under one leg of the stand. And behold, the tree stood.

Hallelujah!

We had several people over to the house that year, and they all commented on how pretty our tree looked and how nice it smelled. As I passed around some goodies, one of them said, "That's a beautiful tree. Was it hard to put up?"

I fixed a smile on my face. "Nah. The whole family helped." I glanced back at our now-well-behaved tree, all sparkly and shiny and happily hovering over our many presents.

Just to spite me, an ornament shivered.

Where is Christmas?

We look in the wrong places.
It's not in the overeating, overindulgent,
Or over-gifted customs we're so fond of.

Christmas is found in the quiet spaces between
hectic events,
In stolen moments,
Where even a few minutes of peace seem so
profound.
It's in an earnest chat with a dear friend,
With quiet smiles and easy rapport.
It's in a grateful whiff of a savory soup
Or the taste of a favorite dessert.
It's watching children or grandchildren sleep,
Their angelic faces swept into sweet dreams.
It's the splendor of a winter sunset,
A full, ivory moon rising above the mountains,
And the soft glow of a handmade luminary.

It's the prayer said

When an Advent candle is lit,

When the travelers arrive safely,

And when we relax,

Knowing that all our loved ones are snug

and safe and warm.

In these things,

We find Christmas, and more.

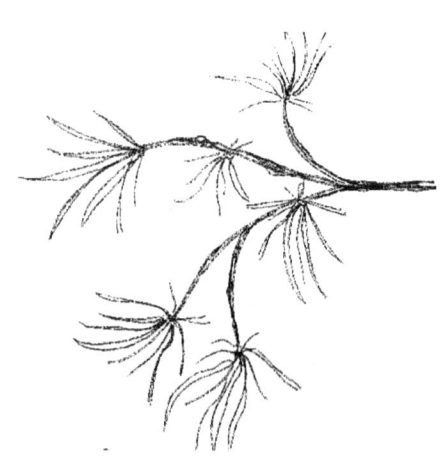

About the author

L. Phillips Carlson has more than 130 published articles, short stories and poems to her credit, most under a different pen name. She also worked as a copy editor for a group of nationally-distributed magazines, wrote and edited a local newsletter for a decade, and penned an award-winning church history. When not writing, Ms. Carlson travels widely, sings in a symphonic chorus, and tends to various members of her family. She lives in sunny New Mexico with her retired-engineer husband in a pueblo-style home they designed themselves.

Also by L. Phillips Carlson:

A Matter of Possession
a paranormal mystery novel

Website:
www.lphillipscarlson.com

Author page:
www.amazon.com/author/lphillipscarlson